ALLY KAZAM'S MAGICAL JOURNEY

THE GINGER PIRATES OF THE FIERY COAST

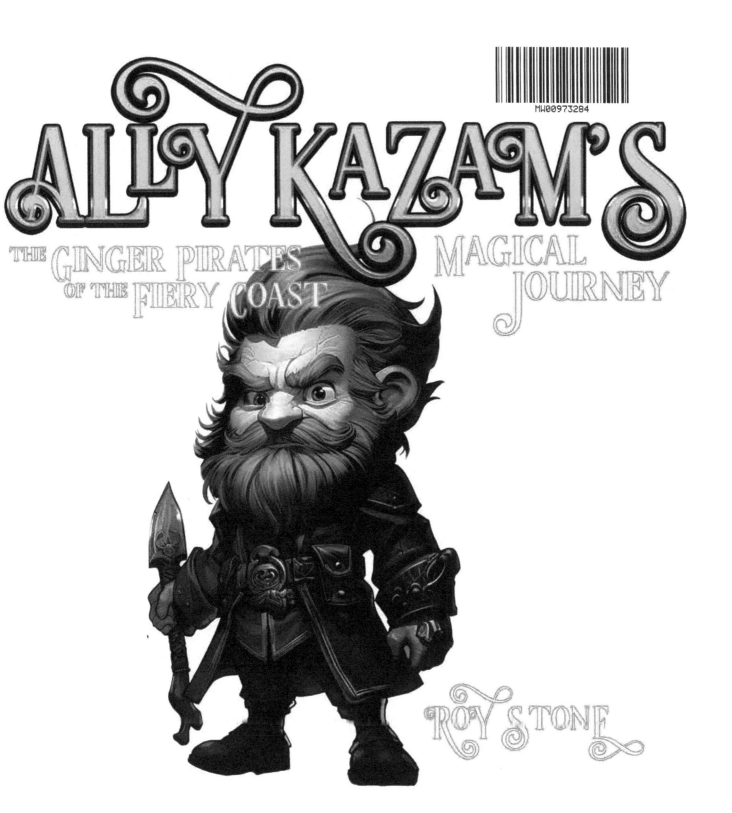

ROY STONE

Ally Kazam's Magical Journey - The Ginger Pirates of The Fiery Coast

Published in the United States by

Roy Stone, Ally Kazam's Magical Journey - The Ginger Pirates of The Fiery Coast

Summary: "Ally Kazam's Magical Journey - TThe Ginger Pirates of The Fiery Coast"

Off the tropical Fiery Coast, the Ginger Pirates catch a lively parrot named Percy and an old tortoise named Tiberius. When they are locked up together, they don't know that their lives will soon be tied together as well. Percy, who is known for being good with fire, and Tiberius, who is known for being good at healing, join forces with Ally Kazam, a young magician's assistant. The pirates want to use Ally's power to open portals to expand their plundering reach. The three people must get away from the pirates and get back home. Another magical journey which demon- strates us how real magic comes from being the heart.

Manufactured in The United States of America

Special thanks to Cari, my awesome wife my concept and proofreader, and for her support in all I do.

David Mitchell for support and his editorial skills.

ALLY KAZAM'S

THE GINGER PIRATES OF THE FIERY COAST

MAGICAL JOURNEY

ROY STONE

Two amazing creatures fell prey to the infamous Ginger Pirates in the bustling center of the Fiery Coast. They had no idea that fate would bring them together for a journey they would never forget.

The beautiful tropical island where Percy, a parrot with colorful plumage, and countless other frolicking birds dwelt was a sight to behold. He flew over the clear blue skies every day, his brightly colored feathers glinting in the sunlight, and took great pleasure in demonstrating his mental fire-starting abilities.

While Percy was up in the sky exploring the island's thick forest one day, he spotted a strange gleam out in the distance. Flying closer out of curiosity, he fell victim to the Ginger Pirates' elaborate trap. A cage fell from a tree branch above trapping him. He tried to use his talent to light the mesh on fire, but it was blocked due to the sound coming from the strange seashells the pirates had attached to the cage. The pirates stepped out of the darkness, their greedy eyes shining at the sight of the parrot. They took Percy captive and locked him up on their ship seeing the potential in his abilities.

Tiberius, the ancient tortoise, lived all his days in peace as the treasured pet of a retired scholar. He would spend his days in a wonderful library, poring over old books and relics. Tiberius often healed his master's ailments with a simple touch from his nose.

In their pursuit of magical artifacts and treasures, the pirates one night broke into the home of the scholar. The elderly guy fought valiantly to protect his home, but he was finally unsuccessful. After investigating the commotion, Tiberius discovered his master laying on the floor, severely injured from multiple wounds. With surprising speed for an elderly reptile, he scurried to the man's side and nuzzled him with his rough beak-like nose. Around each cut, pink rays of light suddenly appeared, offering comfort and healing. Tiberius' extraordinary healing powers were discovered by his captors, who saw the
potential to use his gift for their own nefarious ends. The tortoise was kidnapped and stowed away aboard their ship, where he was kept in a cramped, dark hold, far from the comfort of his loving home.

Confined in the pirates' dark hold, Percy and Tiberius had no idea that their paths were going to cross with Ally Kazam, setting the stage for a magnificent and dangerous adventure in the perilous Fiery Cost.

Percy squawked angrily in the ship's hold, his bright feathers ruffled with anger. "Let me out!" He yelled at the pirates, "You won't get away with this!" hoping to frighten them with his blazing display.

Tiberius, meanwhile, kept his cool, his shrewd eyes watching the unfolding drama with a touch of pity in them. He felt terrible about the innocent people whose lives would be ruined by the abuse of his abilities.

The infamous Ginger Pirates heard rumors of Ally Kazam's magical abilities after they became aware of his growing notoriety. The pirates were so set on using Ally's abilities for themselves that they came up with a diabolical plot to kidnap him and force him into opening a portal to the most heavily guarded treasure vault in the Five Fiery Isles.

During a violent storm, the Ginger Pirates swooped down and attacked, blowing into their conch shells and unleashing a sound wave that neutralized his magic. Ally was sent into deep sleep induced by the noise. When Ally awoke, he discovered that he was sharing a cage with Percy and Tiberius. They were captive together in a cage surrounded by charmed conch shells that all emitted the same magical sound wave, limiting their abilities.

When Ally realized how perilous their situation was, his stomach dropped. Concerned, he inquired, "Who are you both, and how did you end up here?"

The parrot confidently declared, "I'm Percy; captured for my fiery tricks. They have the belief that my fires will lead them to hidden riches."
"And I am Tiberius," the placid turtle continued, "taken for my healing powers. The pirates think they can profit from me because of the abilities I possess."

Ally listened carefully, beginning to grasp the gravity of their situation. If they joined forces, he believed they could escape.
"We have to figure out a way out of here," Ally said, his resolve driving his magic. "Together, we can stop these evil pirates."
With their newfound friendship, Percy, Tiberius, and Ally started to come up with a plan to foil the Ginger Pirates' evil plot.

After spending more time with Percy, Ally noticed a small amount of sap on the bars of their cage. He realized that if Percy could heat them more sap would ooze from the wooden bars of their cage. The three creatures used the sap to create earplugs, shielding themselves from the horrible sound of the shells.

Though not a perfect solution, the sap did allow Ally to make a small portal around the cage lock, causing it to fall off and allowing them to escape despite their diminished abilities.

They were about to get away when a pirate guard caught them by surprise. The three of them fought hard, but their powers got out of hand and set fire to the hold. The fire and the holes made by the wrongly aimed portals did a lot of damage to the ship, and it started to take on water. As the ship went down, the situation got worse, and the magical beings had to move quickly.

Ally, Percy, and Tiberius knew they had to leave the ship, and they looked for a way to get to a nearby island.

They searched and fought their way around the ship until they found the small row bow called a dinghy that the pirates used to get from the ship to the land. Percy went ahead by flying, while Ally and Tiberius took the boat to a nearby island.

When they looked back, they could see the pirates jump off the ship and swim their way to land.

As each of the hated pirates came ashore, they were so tired from fighting and swimming that they were easy to catch and tie up.

Percy started a big fire to keep everyone warm, and Tiberius used his healing powers to tend to the pirates' wounds.

Realizing his ability was finally working correctly again, now that the pirates' shells were safely at the bottom of the ocean Ally opened a portal to the nearest jail and sent the pirates there to face trial for their many crimes.

Now that the danger had been eliminated, it was time to say goodbye to the mystical creatures who had become unexpected friends. Ally created portals leading back to each of their homes, Percy, Tiberius, and Ally said their final goodbyes knowing the hardships they overcame together created a bond that would last a lifetime.

After they said their goodbyes, an exhausted and battle-weary Ally returned through a portal to his own home. When he finally got home, he found the magician who had been looking for him nonstop sitting impatiently at his doorstep.

The magician expressed his relief and thanks for Ally's safe return with a heartfelt embrace as he greeted his companion. Tears of relief welled up in his eyes as he cried out, "Ally!" 'There you are! I've been searching everywhere for you. I was so worried. Where have you been?"

Ally told the story of his dangerous journey, and the magician was impressed by his courage and selflessness.

They discussed the life lessons Aly had picked up along the way. He talked about how they were stronger as a team, how compassion was crucial, and how they had the responsibility to use their powers wisely. The magician was pleased with how his friend had grown stronger and wiser as a result of his adventures. He had proven that the most powerful form of magic is the kindness of one's heart.

Printed in the USA
CPSIA information can be obtained
at www.ICGtesting.com
LVHW070418151124
796625LV00024B/38